Marven of the Great North Woods

WRITTEN BY

Kathryn Lasky

ILLUSTRATED BY

Kevin Hawkes

HARCOURT BRACE & COMPANY   *San Diego   New York   London*

Requests for permission to make copies of any part of the work
should be mailed to: Permissions Department, Harcourt Brace & Company,
6277 Sea Harbor Drive, Orlando, Florida 32887-6777.

Library of Congress Cataloging-in-Publication Data
Lasky, Kathryn.
Marven of the great north woods/written by Kathryn Lasky;
illustrated by Kevin Hawkes.
p. cm.
Summary: When his Jewish parents send him to a Minnesota logging camp to
escape the influenza epidemic of 1918, ten-year-old Marven finds a special friend.
ISBN 0-15-200104-2
[1. Lumber camps—Fiction. 2. Loggers—Fiction. 3. Influenza—Fiction.
4. Jews—Minnesota—Fiction.] I. Hawkes, Kevin, ill. II. Title.
PZ7.L3274Mar 1997
[E]—dc20 96-2334

C E F D B

Printed in Singapore

The illustrations in this book were done in acrylic on acid-free museum board.
The display type was set in Goudy Mediaeval and the text type was set in Granjon
by Harcourt Brace & Company Photocomposition Center, San Diego, California.
Color separations by Bright Arts, Ltd., Singapore
Printed and bound by Tien Wah Press, Singapore
This book was printed on totally chlorine-free Nymolla Matte Art paper.
Production supervision by Stanley Redfern and Pascha Gerlinger
Designed by Lori McThomas Buley

After his great-aunt Sadie died of the influenza, Marven's mother and father decided to send him away from the city to keep him safe. Marven heard them talk it over with Uncle Moishe and Aunt Ghisa one night as he sat hidden on the stairs.

"How will he get along in a logging camp? A boy of ten, all by himself?" asked Aunt Ghisa.

"I want him to live to be a man," said Mama quietly. "He must go."

"But Marven's very small for his age," said Uncle Moishe. "He won't even be able to lift a saw." Marven glowered and huddled closer to the wall.

"He's got a head for numbers. He'll keep the books," said Papa. Marven knew that he was good at math in school. But a logging camp? "I've already talked to my friend Mr. Murray at the camp up north," Papa continued. "Marven should go right away."

The next day Marven's mother cut down an old overcoat of Papa's and lined it with scraps of beaver fur. From the scraps of the scraps, she lined Marven's cap and made earflaps.

Marven turned to his mother. "Mama, I don't know how to speak French. You said most of the men who work there are French Canadian, except for Mr. Murray."

"You just say *bonjour*."

"*Bonjour*," Marven repeated.

"It means hello," Mama said. "You'll learn the rest. Like your father and I did when we came from Russia."

"Your mother's right," said Papa. "Look, we are living proof. When we came here, not a word of English. Just Russian and Yiddish. Now look at us. We talk English to all our children. I talk English to my boss. We sing in English. We make jokes in English."

Marven hoped his father wouldn't tell the chicken joke. It was a dumb joke.

Two days later, the morning Marven was to leave, Mama made latkes and knishes. While they were piping hot, she wrapped them in newspaper and put two in each of his coat pockets and one inside his cap to keep him warm.

"Don't eat them until they're almost cold," she told him. "Then they'll warm you twice."

At the train station, Papa handed Marven the skis he had made for his son's sixth birthday.

"Papa, I've never skied in the country before," Marven said anxiously.

"You've skied in the city. Up and down every hill in Duluth, and there are many."

"How far do I have to ski?"

"Five miles, remember? It's all flat. You'll go like a shot."

The train pulled out of the station, and the glass grew foggy with Marven's breath as he said soft good-byes through the window. Would his family be all right until he came home in the spring? He wished he could take his sisters to the logging camp to keep them safe from the influenza, too. He saw them all there on the platform—Mama, Papa, his two big sisters, his two little sisters—bundled in their coats, waving. As the train moved away, the little sisters blurred into the big ones; the big sisters blended into Papa and Mama. They were all one bundle waving good-bye to him—Marven, alone on the train, going far, far away to the great north woods.

Marven ate his first latke when the train stopped in Floodwood. It was almost cold. An hour passed, and Marven ate another latke, then another. Outside, the land stretched white until it reached the trees. The dark band of the forest rested on the horizon as the train sped through the white world of the north.

Almost five hours later, in Bemidji, Minnesota, Marven stood alone on the platform as the train rolled away. Beyond the depot a road ran straight and flat to where the white landscape met the forest. Marven felt small, very small, and the road looked like it went on forever. He thought of the big waving bundle on the train platform back in Duluth. What were they doing now—his sisters, his mother, his father?

It was too cold to stand still. So Marven ate the knish in his cap, slapped his cap back on his head, strapped on his skis, and started for the shadowy thread on the horizon. His father had told him that five miles down the road, Mr. Murray, a very big man with a handsome waxed mustache, would be waiting for him.

The way was flat and the snow was well packed. Marven thought that if he kept up a good pace, he would reach the camp just after sunset. The thin thread of the forest thickened to a dark ribbon.

Soon he could smell the sharp green fragrance of freshly cut timber, and soon after that he spotted a speck in the distance. The speck grew into a smudge; before long the smudge wore a muffler and a fur hat. Between the top of the muffler and the bottom of the hat, a huge mustache bristled with frost.

"Come along, boy." Mr. Murray turned his snowshoes toward the camp at the edge of the forest. "I'm like to freeze my *derrière* off. That's French for 'bottom.'"

So, Marven thought, *now I know two words in French. I can say, "Hello, bottom."*

As they entered the camp, the longest shadows Marven had ever
seen stretched across the snow, and he realized with a start that the
shadows were the lumberjacks walking in the moonlight. He could
smell hay and manure and saw the silhouettes of horses stomping in a
snowy corral. From a nearby log building he heard the lively squeaks
of a fiddle. It seemed for a moment as if the horses were keeping time
to the music. Mr. Murray must have thought the same. "You want to
watch the horses dance, or the jacks?" He laughed. "Come along, we'll
take a look."

When they entered the building, the long shadows from the yard
suddenly sprung to life. Marven stared. Immense men with long
beards and wild hair were jumping around to the fiddler's tunes like a
pack of frantic grizzly bears. They were the biggest and wildest men
Marven had ever seen.

Marven could have watched the dancing all night, but Mr. Murray
said, "Come on, Marven. We start early in the morning. I'll show you
where you'll be living."

Mr. Murray took Marven to the small office where he would work and sleep. In Duluth, Marven had to share a bedroom with his two younger sisters and all of their dolls and toys, but this room was his— all his—and he liked it. A bed with a bearskin on it sat across from a woodstove; nearby, wood was stacked neatly. The big desk had cubbyholes for papers, envelopes, glue pots, and blotter strips. And on the desk there were blocks of paper and a big black ledger. There were pencils in a blue glass jar, as well as an inkwell. Marven hoped that somewhere there was a very good pen—a fountain pen.

"In addition to keeping the payroll," Mr. Murray said, "you have another job. The first bell in the morning is at four o'clock; second bell at four-fifteen. Third bell is at four-twenty. By four-twenty-five, if any jack is still in the sack, he's *en retard,* 'late.' So you, son, are the fourth bell. Starting tomorrow, you go into the bunkhouse and wake *les en retard*s."

"How?"

"You tap them on the shoulder, give 'em a shake, scream in their ear if you have to."

Then Mr. Murray said good night, and Marven was alone again.

It seemed to Marven he had just crawled under the bearskin when he heard the first bell. The fire was out and the room was cold and dark. He lit the kerosene lamp and pulled on his double-thick long underwear, two pairs of socks, two pairs of knickers, and two sweaters. Then he put on his cut-down overcoat.

After the second bell, Marven heard the jacks heading toward the eating hall. It was nearly time for his first job.

He ran through the cold morning darkness to the bunkhouse, peeked in, and counted five huge lumps in the shadows. Five jacks in the sacks. Marven waited just inside the door.

At the third bell, Marven was relieved to see two jacks climb out of bed. He thought there must be a *broche,* a Hebrew blessing, for something like this. His father knew all sorts of *broches*—blessings for seeing the sunrise, blessings for the first blossom of spring. Was there a *broche* for a rising lumberjack? If he said a *broche,* maybe the other three would get up on their own.

One lump stirred, then another. They grunted, rolled, and climbed out from under the covers. Their huge shadows slid across the ceiling.

One jack was still in the sack. Marven took a deep breath, walked bravely over to the bed, reached out, and tapped the jack's shoulder. It was like poking a granite boulder. The jack's beard ran right into his long, shaggy hair; Marven couldn't even find an ear to shout into. He cupped his hands around his mouth and leaned forward.

"Up!"

The jack grunted and muttered something in French.

"Get up," Marven pleaded.

Another jack pulled on his boots, boomed, "*Lève-toi!* Jean Louis. *Lève-toi,*" and shuffled out the door.

"*Lève-toi!* Jean Louis. *Lève-toi,*" Marven repeated.

Jean Louis opened one eye. It glittered like a blue star beneath his thick black eyebrow. He squinted, as if trying to make out the shape in front of him, then blinked and sat up.

"*Bonjour,*" Marven whispered.

"*Qui es tu? Quel est ton nom?*"

"I don't speak French—just *bonjour, derrière,* and *lève-toi.*"

"That's all? No more?" The man opened his eyes wide now. "So what is your name?"

"Marven."

"Ah…Marven," Jean Louis repeated, as if tasting the sound of his name.

"Will you get up?" Marven asked anxiously.

Jean Louis growled and fixed him in the hard blue squint of one eye.

"Please." Marven stood straight and tried not to tremble.

Jean Louis grunted and swung his feet from beneath the covers. They were as big as skillets, and one of his huge toenails was bruised black and blue. Marven tried not to stare.

Marven and Jean Louis were the last to arrive at the breakfast table. The only sounds were those of chewing and the clink of forks and knives against the plates. At each place were three stacks of flapjacks, one big steak, eight strips of bacon, and a bowl of oatmeal. In the middle of the table were bowls of potatoes and beans with molasses, platters with pies and cakes, and blue jugs filled with tea, coffee, and milk.

Marven stared at the food in dismay. *It's not kosher,* he thought. In Marven's house it was against ancient Jewish law to eat dairy products and meat together. And never, ever, did a Jew eat bacon. Marven came to a quick decision. One day he would eat the flapjacks and oatmeal with milk. The next day he would eat the steak and the oatmeal without milk. And never the bacon.

After breakfast, as they did every morning, the jacks went to the toolhouse to get their saws and axes. Then, wearing snowshoes and pulling huge sleds piled with equipment, they made their way into the great woods, where they would work all day.

Marven went directly to his office after breakfast. Mr. Murray was already there, setting out Marven's work. A fresh pot of ink was thawing in a bowl of hot water on the woodstove. There were two boxes on the desk filled with scraps of paper.

"Cord chits," Mr. Murray said. "The jacks are paid according to the number of cords they cut in a pay period—two weeks. You figure it out. I'm no good as a bookkeeper and have enough other things to do around here. Each chit should have the jack's name—or, if he can't write, his symbol."

"His symbol?" Marven asked weakly.

"Yes. Jean Louis's is a thumbprint. Here's one!" He held up a small piece of paper with a thumbprint on it the size of a baby's fist. Marven blinked.

It was all very confusing. Sometimes two names were on one chit. These were called doublees; there were even some triplees. This meant more calculations. And sometimes chits were in the wrong pay-period box.

Marven sat staring at the scraps. "There is no system!" he muttered. Where to begin? His mother always made a list when she had many things to do. So first Marven listed the jacks' names alphabetically and noted the proper symbol for those who could not write. Then he listed the dates of a single pay period, coded each chit with the dates, and, with a ruler, made a chart. By the end of the morning, Marven had a system and knew the name or symbol for each man. There were many chits with the huge thumbprint of Jean Louis.

Every day Marven worked until midday, when he went into the cookhouse and ate baked beans and two kinds of pie with Mr. Murray and the cook. After lunch he returned to his office and worked until the jacks returned from the forest for supper.

By Friday of the second week, Marven had learned his job so well that he finished early. He had not been on his skis since he had arrived at camp. Every day the routine was simply meals and work, and Marven kept to his office and away from the lumberjacks as much as he could. But today he wanted to explore, so he put on his skis and followed the sled paths into the woods.

He glided forward, his skis making soft whisking sounds in the snow. This certainly was different from city skiing in Duluth, where he would dodge the ragman's cart or the milkman's wagon, where the sky was notched with chimney pots belching smoke, where the snow turned sooty as soon as it fell.

Here in the great north woods all was still and white. Beads of ice glistened on bare branches like jewels. The frosted needles of pine and spruce pricked the eggshell sky, and a ghostly moon began to climb over the treetops.

Marven came upon a frozen lake covered with snow, which lay in a circle of tall trees like a bowl of sugar. He skimmed out across it on his skis, his cheeks stinging in the cold air, and stopped in the middle to listen to the quietness.

And then Marven heard a deep, low growl. At the edge of the lake a shower of snow fell from a pine. A grizzly bear? Marven gripped his ski poles. A grizzly awake in the winter! What would he do if a bear came after him? Where could he hide? Could he out-ski a grizzly?

Marven began to tremble, but he knew that he must remain still, very still. Maybe, Marven thought desperately, the grizzly would think he was a small tree growing in the middle of the lake. He tried very hard to look like a tree. But concentrating on being a tree was difficult because Marven kept thinking of the bundle on the train platform— his mother, his father, his two big sisters, his two little sisters. He belonged in Duluth with them, not in the middle of the great north woods with a grizzly. The hot tears streaming down his cheeks turned cold, then froze.

When another tree showered snow, Marven, startled, shot out
across the lake. As he reached the shore, a huge shadow slid from
behind the trees. The breath froze in Marven's throat.

In the thick purple shadows, he saw a blue twinkle.

"Aaah! Marven!" Jean Louis held a glistening ax in one hand.
He looked taller than ever. "I mark the tree for cutting next season."
He stepped closer to the trunk and swung the ax hard. Snow showered
at Marven's feet.

"Ah, *mon petit,* you cry!" Jean Louis took off his glove and rubbed his huge thumb down Marven's cheek. "You miss your mama? Your papa?" Marven nodded silently.

"Jean Louis," he whispered. The huge lumberjack bent closer. "I thought you were a grizzly bear!"

"You what!" Jean Louis gasped. "You think I was a grizzly!" And Jean Louis began to laugh, and as he roared, more snow fell from the tree, for his laugh was as powerful as his ax.

As they made their way back to the sled paths, Marven heard a French song drifting through the woods. The other jacks came down the path, their saws and axes slung across their shoulders, and Marven and Jean Louis joined them. Evening shadows fell through the trees, and as Marven skied alongside the huge men, he hummed the tune they were singing.

One day followed the next. Every morning, in that time when the night had worn thin but the day had not yet dawned, Marven shouted, "Up! *Lève-toi! Lève-toi!*" to Jean Louis. Together they would go to the dining hall, where one day Marven would eat steak and oatmeal without milk; the next day he would eat oatmeal with milk and flapjacks but no steak. Jean Louis always ate the bacon and anything else Marven left.

And every afternoon after that, Marven would finish his work well before sunset and ski into the woods. Although the worry that his family might catch the terrible sickness nagged at him constantly, when he was in the woods his fears grew dim in the silence and shadows of the winter forest. And every day he would fall in beside Jean Louis as the jacks returned to camp, and he would hum the French songs that Jean Louis told him were about a beautiful woman in the far, far north, or a lonely bear in its den, or a lovely maiden named Go With Clouds.

At night, after supper was done, Marven learned the lumberjacks'
songs and how to play their games—the ones he could manage, like ax
throwing. A jack would heave an ax from thirty paces at the tail end
of a log; for Marven they moved the mark up to ten feet. The jacks
challenged each other to barrel lifting and bucksaw contests, but
Marven was too small for those.

He was not, however, too small to dance. Sometimes he danced on
the floor, and sometimes Jean Louis lifted him and Marven did a little
two-step right there in his stocking feet on the shoulders of the big
lumberjack.

In April, four months after Marven had arrived at the camp, the snow began to melt. Mr. Murray said to Marven, "I promised your parents I'd send you back while there was still enough snow for you to ski on. Every day it grows warmer. You better go before you have to swim out of here. I'll send your parents a letter to say you're coming home. But I don't know what I'll do for a bookkeeper."

So it was planned that Marven would leave on the last day of the month. When the day came, he went to the bunkhouse to find Jean Louis.

"Ah, Marven." Jean Louis tasted Marven's name as he had the first time he had ever said it, as if it were the most delicious French pastry in the world. "I have something for you, *mon petit*." He got up and opened the chest at the end of his bed.

"You are a woodsman now," he said, and handed Marven a brand-new ax. The head was sharp and glinting; the handle glistened like dark honey.

"*Merci,* Jean Louis. *Merci beaucoup,*" Marven whispered.

Jean Louis went with Marven all the way to the train station. When the snow ran out on the banks of a muddy creek near the depot, he turned to Marven, grinned widely, and said, "Up, up. *Lève-toi,* Marven." The giant of a man swung the small boy onto his shoulders, skis and all, and carried him across to the opposite bank.

As the train pulled away, Marven waved at Jean Louis through the window, which had become foggy with his breath. "*Au revoir,*" he murmured. "*Au revoir,* Jean Louis."

Marven sat alone on the train and thought of his family. Who would be waiting for him at the station? He felt the edge of his new ax. It was so sharp, so bright. But it was good only for cutting wood. What could it do against the terrible flu that had sent him away?

With each mile the land slid out from under its snowy cover. When the train finally pulled into the station in Duluth, Marven pressed his face against the window, the glass fogging as he searched the crowd on the platform.

When Marven stepped down from the train he was still searching. Everyone looked pale and winter worn, and not a single face was familiar. Then suddenly he was being smothered with kisses and hugs. His little sisters were grabbing him around his waist, his big sisters were kissing his ears, and then all of them tumbled into Mama's and Papa's arms, and they were one big hugging bundle.

"You're not dead!" Marven said. His sisters, Mama, Papa, Aunt Ghisa, and Uncle Moishe crowded around him in a tight circle. He turned slowly to look at each face.

"Nobody's dead," Marven repeated softly.

"The sickness is over," said Mama. "And you are finally home!"

A NOTE FROM THE AUTHOR

Marven at age ten

Marven Lasky was born in 1907 in Duluth, Minnesota. He was the first child born in America to Ida and Joseph Lasky, who had emigrated from Tsarist Russia to escape the persecution of Jews. The story of their escape in 1900 was told in my novel *The Night Journey.*

In 1918 an influenza epidemic swept through the United States. The disease was the worst in the cities, among large populations. Old people and young children were the most vulnerable. Ida and Joseph believed that they might save at least one of their children if they could arrange for that child to go far from the city. Marven was not chosen because he was loved most; Joseph and Ida loved all of their children. Girls in that era, however, were never permitted to travel far from home by themselves—and the last place a girl would ever be sent was to a logging camp. Marven, therefore, was sent by himself on a train to a logging camp in the great north woods of Minnesota.

Marven in his late sixties

Marven Lasky, my father, is now more than ninety years old. The last time he skied was at age eighty-three in Aspen, Colorado. He still has a good head for figures.